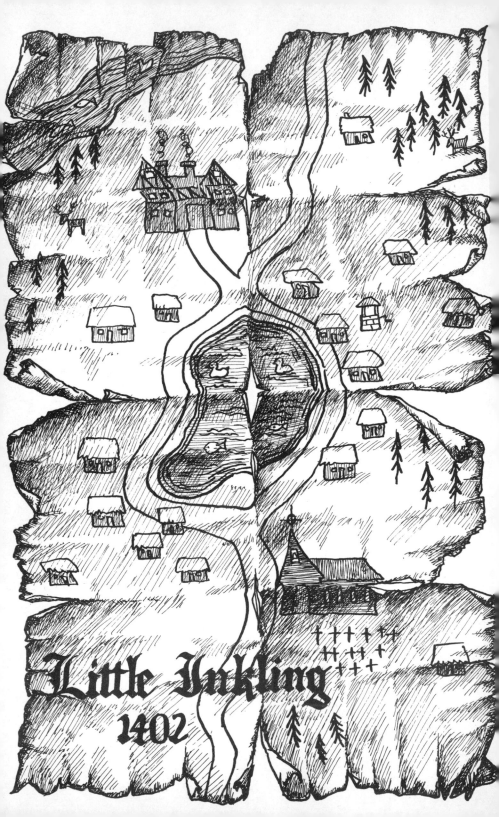

Little Inkling

1402

A
WITCH
IN TIME

TERRY DEARY

ILLUSTRATED BY
P.J. LYNCH

A & C BLACK • LONDON

Black Cats

The Ramsbottom Rumble • Georgia Byng
Calamity Kate • Terry Deary
The Custard Kid • Terry Deary
The Ghosts of Batwing Castle • Terry Deary
Ghost Town • Terry Deary
Into the Lion's Den • Terry Deary
The Joke Factory • Terry Deary
The Treasure of Crazy Horse • Terry Deary
The Wishing Well Ghost • Terry Deary
A Witch in Time • Terry Deary
Dear Ms • Joan Poulson
It's a Tough Life • Jeremy Strong
Big Iggy • Kaye Umansky
Something Slimy on Primrose Drive • Karen Wallace

First paperback edition 2002
First published in hardback 1986 by
A & C Black Publishers Ltd
37 Soho Square, London W1D 3QZ
www.acblack.com

ISBN 0-7136-6202-6

A CIP record for this book is available from the
British Library.

A & C Black uses paper produced with elemental
chlorine-free pulp, harvested from managed sustainable forests.

Printed and bound in Spain by G. Z. Printek, Bilbao.

Little Inkling 1402

The village of Little Inkling was quiet. It was so quiet that you could have heard the dust settling on the daisies round the village pond.

The warm September air was suddenly ruffled by a pattering of small feet. A young girl scuttered on to the village green and looked around wildly. The sun's rays and the dust of the fields had turned her face as brown as oak wood. Her hair was dark and as tangled as a bramble bush.

A heavy cloud covered the sun; the air turned suddenly cool and a large blob of rain struck the girl on the cheek. She cried as if the raindrop had been a slap. 'Oh! They'll say it was my fault!'

She looked at the white cottages standing round the green. Dark windows, like hooded eyes, stared back at her blankly. Not a single friendly face in all the village, she thought . . . well, maybe one.

Granny Rickles' tumbledown cottage!

The girl looked over her shoulder. They weren't coming to get her yet . . . but they would.

She lifted the latch of Granny Rickles' door and called, 'Hello! It's me . . . Eleanor Nash . . . can I come in?'

From a pile of dirty straw in the corner an old voice grated, 'What does a little witch-child like you want with me?'

The old woman sat in the straw, her face as brown and wrinkled as a walnut shell. Ellie started to gabble her story. 'The villagers have just cut the hay on the common,' she gasped. 'They told me to go away . . . but I wanted to help Dad . . they'd just finished when I saw the storm clouds over the hills. It's raining now! The hay will be ruined – half the cattle will starve this winter – and they'll blame me!'

The old woman nodded her head. 'Witchcraft,' she mumbled.

'But I'm *not* a witch!' Ellie cried. 'I'm really not!'

Granny Rickles shook her head and sucked air past her single yellow tooth. 'You may *think* you're not a witch,' she croaked, 'yet still be a child of the devil.'

A flash of lightning lit up the dingy room and made three chickens run to hide in the straw.

The girl moaned. 'If their hay is ruined they'll kill me this time . . . even if it isn't my fault, they'll have to find someone to blame. They'll burn me!'

The rumble of thunder mingled with the rumbling tramp of heavy, angry men and boys. Ellie made for the gap in the back wall of the cottage that served as a window. She pushed the sacking aside and was about the climb out when Granny Rickles cried, 'Nay, lass, wait here till the rain stops.'

A roll of thunder sounded like someone hammering on the door; then a hammering on the door came like thunder. Ellie gasped.

The old woman bounced to her feet like a rag ball. 'Hide, lass. Quick.'

The girl looked around the bare room. 'Where?' she whispered.

The thundering knock was repeated. 'Granny Rickles!' boomed a voice. 'Have you seen anything of the Nash child? We think she came this way!'

The old woman waved to a pile of dirty straw in the corner of the room. 'Under my bedstraw!' she hissed. Ellie hid quickly while her rescuer hobbled to the door.

The straw tickled her nose and the smell made her feel ill. But all she had to do was hold her breath for a minute or two. Old Mrs Rickles was talking to a man at the door. Through the hissing rain that dripped through the thatch roof Ellie could hear most of what was being said.

'Now, Harry Henson, what do you want? Waking an old woman just as she was settling down of an evening,' Granny Rickles was grumbling.

'We're after that young Eleanor Nash,' the man replied.

'What's she done this time?' the old woman whined.

'Ruined a good hay crop, that's what,' Henson said, his voice lower now, and more menacing. 'If we don't find young Ellie Nash soon the others will be getting impatient. They're so angry, they'd burn anyone at the moment . . . even you!'

A chicken found the girl under the straw and settled against her face. The feathers of its wing made her want to sneeze. She wanted to shake it off but didn't dare move.

Granny Rickles was sniffling miserably and tugging at the blacksmith's leather jerkin. 'You wouldn't harm poor old Mary Rickles, would you Harry? You wouldn't let them, would you?'

'If we don't find Ellie Nash soon then I may not be able to stop them,' the blacksmith rumbled.

There was a silence that lasted about six heartbeats then the girl heard old Granny Rickles say softly, 'You'll find her underneath my bedstraw . . .'

2

Father Seyton

Ellie stumbled from the straw and dived through the hole in the back wall of the cottage. She landed in a bed of purple nettles and sent a cloud of orange butterflies shimmering into the grey skies. The cold rain cooled the nettle stings, but Ellie hadn't time to notice them anyway. The pink face of Harry Henson poked through the sack curtain. His short brown hair bristled like a scrubbing brush. 'Come here, witch-child,' he growled.

Ellie shook her head dumbly. Henson's fat, hairy hand shot out and grasped her skinny arm but the rain made it slippery and she was able to tear herself free. She scrambled to her feet and ran.

Henson looked at the nettles and then back into the cottage. 'She's made a run for it. She'll try to get home to Nash's farm. Head her off!'

Ellie had reached the churchyard wall by the time the men burst from the front of the cottage. There were five of them, led by Harry Henson. She felt sure that she could reach home before they caught her . . . until she saw that they weren't chasing straight after her. They had gone to the far side of the village pond and blocked the road they knew she would have to take.

Ellie stopped and panted painfully. The cold rain on her face gave her a welcome drink, but fear made her throat too tight to swallow it. The men watched her carefully then slowly walked towards her. Ellie backed away, trying to keep the pond between herself and her enemies. But Henson saw her plan. He sent two men round the right side of the pond while he led the others round the left. Like a pair of pincers they would catch her between them.

Ellie kept walking backwards, never taking her eyes off the men. At last she felt the damp stone wall against her back and knew there was no place left to run. She began to edge her way along the wall. There was no thought in her mind except what it would be like to be burned as a witch.

Her movement made Henson stop. He cried suddenly in a wild, hoarse voice, 'The church! Stop her, lads ... she's heading for the church! Stop her before she gets there!'

The men tried to run but slithered on the damp moss at the edge of the pond.

'The church?' Ellie thought. 'Why are they afraid that I might go into the church?'

Suddenly the answer came to her. 'Sanctuary! Of course.' She'd heard about that before. If a criminal could reach a church before he was captured then he could stay there safely ... the law couldn't touch him. The law officers just had to wait until the criminal came out.

Perhaps it was the same for witches, Ellie thought.

Ellie heard Henson's cry of rage as she ducked through the church gateway and hurried past grey gravestones up the path to the door. She put her shoulder to the studded oak door and pushed. It swung open silently and she slipped into the gloomy church.

At first it was too dark to make out anything, but as her eyes became used to the light she was able to see a shadowy shape by the altar. A man in a faded black robe was taking the altar cross from its base and setting it the right way up. He pulled some dark candles from their holders and put fresh white ones in their place. When he had lit one Ellie was able to make out his face.

It was an ugly face. The stringy brown beard didn't hide the thin, wet lips. The flickering candlelight glinted on the bulging, watery blue eyes. Eyes that seemed to look into Ellie's soul every Sunday in church.

'Good afternoon, Father Seyton,' Ellie said.

'Who's that?' the priest said sharply. He pushed the old candles quickly behind the choir stall. He strode down the aisle of the church towards the girl. His robes flapped like the tattered wings of a dying bat and Ellie was afraid. She couldn't remember a time when she hadn't been afraid of Father Seyton. His Sunday sermons about sinners and the devil burning them in Hell gave her more nightmares than she cared to remember.

'Ah . . . Eleanor . . . Eleanor Nash, isn't it?' His voice was calm and smooth now but the girl noticed that the candle flame flickered as his hand shook slightly.

'Sorry I startled you, Father,' she muttered.

'No . . . child . . . I was just praying,' he said and his mouth stretched in a cold smile.

Ellie was puzzled. For Father Seyton *hadn't* been praying. He'd been tidying the church. She'd seen him. But he couldn't have been lying to her . . . priests don't lie, she thought. She must have been mistaken.

'What can I do for you?' he asked, holding the candle so close to her face that she could feel its warmth.

'I want the shelter of the church, please Father,' she said quickly. 'Harry Henson and some of the other men are chasing me . . .'

'And why would they want to do that?' Father Seyton asked.

'Because she's a witch-child!' came a harsh voice from the back of the church.

Ellie swung round to see the men darken the doorway. 'I'm not!' she cried.

Father Seyton turned on his booming sermon voice. 'That is a serious charge, Harry Henson... can you prove it?'

'Aye,' the man muttered. 'There's been a curse on this village ever since that girl was born... the crops have been bad, animals have gone sick... and there have been odd accidents.'

'But can you prove that young Eleanor is to blame?' Father Seyton said.

'None of those things have happened to the Nash family, have they?' Henson spat. 'The witch-child's father grows fatter while we grow thinner... the curse doesn't affect him. That *proves* it's her!'

Father Seyton shook his shaggy head. 'No, Harry. You can't burn the child just because her father has been luckier than the rest of you.'

'That's right,' Ellie said. 'Dad's better off than you because he works harder than you and he's a better farmer.'

The girl's words just made Henson angrier than ever. He stepped forward boldly. 'Are you defending the little witch, Father Seyton?' he growled.

The priest seemed to take a step back and his voice took on an unpleasant whine. 'No, Harry, no! I'm just saying that before you can burn her you have to give her a trial.'

'A trial? How could we do that?'

'Well, the easiest witch trial is trial by ducking,' Father Seyton said.

'Aye,' Henson muttered. 'I remember we did that to an old man when I was just a boy. You tie the witch hand and foot, don't you Father?'

'That's right,' the priest nodded. His tongue flickered over his lips. 'Then throw them into the nearest pond ... if the witch floats then they are guilty of the crime of witchcraft ... you take them out and burn them.'

'But what if I sink?' Ellie asked with a shudder.

'If you sink then you're innocent. You are not a witch and you are free to go,' Father Seyton said.

'But if I sink I'll drown!' Ellie cried.

The priest shrugged. 'Perhaps ... but at least your soul may go to heaven.' Suddenly the priest's hand gripped her shoulder and he said, 'Here, Harry, take her to the pond ... it'll be nicely full after the storm.'

Henson walked towards her. Ellie screamed and wriggled. She tore herself away from the priest and ran to the altar. She grabbed the large black book that lay there and held it in front of her like a shield. Father Seyton froze; his face turned yellow-grey as he stared at her. Even Harry Henson stopped for a moment. 'You can't touch me – not while I'm holding the holy book!' Ellie sobbed.

'Aye, but you can't stay there forever,' Henson sneered. 'We can wait, witch-child.'

'You'll have a long wait,' the girl shouted.

'I'll wait till fourteen-oh-three if I have to!'

'You can go away... you won't get me if you wait till two thousand and three!'

A raindrop trickled down Ellie's matted hair. She blinked it away.

And when, an instant later, she opened her eyes ... she was alone.

Father Seyton, Harry Henson and the other villagers had vanished.

Ellie sank weakly to the step of the altar and clutched the black book to her damp dress.

'Well!' she said.

3

Sharon Neale. Inkling Village 2003

Sharon Neale tumbled through the door of Inkling Village church. She closed it softly behind her and leaned against it, panting. After a minute or two she opened it carefully and peered out. The September wind snatched at the voices of the boys and carried them to her.

'Try the church,' one cried. She knew that was the voice of Nigel Bennett. 'Just the sort of place Miss Goody-Goody would hide!'

'No ... the church closed ten years ago,' Barry Potter's voice answered. 'She's probably at school by now.'

'Come on then,' Nigel yelled as he turned and ran away from Sharon's hiding place. 'We might be able to get her before the bell goes.'

The clattering feet faded and the angry voices drifted into silence. Sharon leaned against the door and sighed. Of course she knew *why* these two boys hated her ... it was because whenever Miss Dennison asked a question in class Sharon always had the answer. 'But it isn't *my* fault I'm clever and they're stupid,' she thought. 'What am I supposed to do? Pretend to be as simple as they are? Get all the answers wrong so they will stop picking on me?'

She shook her head sadly and began to wander down the aisle of the old church. If she waited here for just ten minutes more then she could slip into school safely just after the bell.

Sharon tightened the blue ribbon in her fair pony-tail and turned up her short nose at the musty smell of the disused church. She had always wanted to explore the building but it had been locked every time she came. For some reason the door had been open today . . . and she was thankful that it had been.

The morning sun shone a rainbow of colours through the stained glass window above the altar. Beams of poppy red and cornflower blue, apple green and buttercup yellow made swirling patterns in the dust.

Then Sharon gave a shiver of fear. For a few moments she didn't know what had made her afraid – then she worked it out.

If the church was disused then the dust should have settled a long time ago.

From the corner of her eye Sharon saw a slight movement. Just a shadow – or perhaps the shadow of a shadow, over by the choir stall.

'Come out!' Sharon cried. She tried to sound fierce but her voice came out like the squeak of a scared squirrel.

Slowly a bush of wild, wet hair rose from the stall. Then a pair of bright blue blinking eyes. Finally Sharon found herself looking into the frightened face of a girl about her own age.

'Are you the devil?' the frightened face asked.

'No!' replied the startled Sharon. 'Are you?'

The wild head of hair shook. 'No, Miss, I'm Eleanor Nash, Miss.'

'And I'm Sharon . . . Sharon Neale. Pleased to meet you Eleanor . . . but what are you doing here?'

'Please, mistress, I'm running away from Harry Henson the blacksmith and his gang . . . they say I'm a witch and they want to burn me!' Ellie Nash said with a sad sniffle.

Sharon laughed softly. 'Don't be silly . . . no one believes in witches in 2003!'

Ellie turned pale – as pale as she could under the sun-baked dust. 'You mean... I'm in the year 2003?' she managed to say in a pitiful croak.

'September 2003,' Sharon nodded.

Ellie sank on to the altar steps. She wrapped her thin arms around the black book. 'Perhaps they're right, then,' she whispered. 'Perhaps I really am a witch!'

Sharon sat next to the trembling girl. 'Tell me about it.'

So Ellie told Sharon the story.

Sharon didn't know how it could be true – yet somehow she knew that Ellie wasn't lying.

Ellie finished her story, 'Then I said, "You won't get me if you wait till *two thousand* and three."... and here I am, in 2003! I think it's something to do with this Bible – and with me being a witch!'

Sharon nodded, her pony-tail bobbing. 'Perhaps it has got something to do with the book you're holding – but that isn't a Bible,' she said slowly.

'But it has a cross on the front,' Ellie exclaimed, pointing to a gold cross on the black leather cover.

'No, the cross is upside down . . . I think that's a sign of witchcraft,' Sharon said.

Ellie dropped the book as if it were an electric eel. 'Witchcraft!' she gasped. 'You mean there is witchcraft in the village?'

'Oh yes . . . there is – I mean maybe there *was*

somebody trying to be a witch in your village.'

'Who?' Ellie asked. 'Granny Rickles?'

Sharon chewed her lip and frowned. She was just about to answer when the church bell began steadily chiming nine o'clock. 'Listen, Ellie, I have to go now . . .'

'You're leaving me?' Ellie cried.

'Just for a few hours . . . I have to go to school,' Sharon explained. Ellie's sea-blue eyes looked blank. 'You'll be safe here,' Sharon told her.

'But . . . I mean . . . what about Harry Henson?'

'He's been dead for nearly six hundred years, I expect,' Sharon said quickly, then she saw that the thought made the slim girl shiver. Sharon had spoken too quickly as usual. She stretched out a hand and touched Ellie's shoulder. The rough brown material was still damp with six-hundred year old rain. 'Don't worry – you can easily get back to your own time; just hold the book and say the year you want to go to – that seems to be the way the magic works.'

Ellie nodded. 'But if I go back then Henson will be waiting for me .. seven people saw me disappear ... that would prove to them that I have witch powers!'

'Yes,' Sharon agreed. 'That's why I want to help you. There may be a way to send you back *and* make sure you're safe – but I need time to think about it.'

The church clock had finished its chiming and Sharon hurried down the aisle.

'I'll be back when the clock strikes twelve,' she called. 'I'll tell you then who your village witch is and how you may be able to prove it.' Sharon looked back to see Ellie on the altar steps. The light through the stained glass window glowed in her hair like a rainbow halo.

For just a little while Sharon had been able to forget her own problems ... now she had to go and face them.

4

Barry Potter

Miss Dennison glared at Sharon over the top of her spectacles. The teacher's short hair was colourless as porridge and her thin face pale as sour milk. 'It's not like you to be late, Sharon Neale.'

'No Miss, sorry Miss,' Sharon muttered. She edged her way to her seat amid the boys' sniggers.

'Not like teacher's pet to be late,' Mark Jones hissed as she passed him. His fat face glowed.

Sharon felt her face burning with shame and anger. As she sat down a slip of paper floated over her shoulder and settled on her desk. A message. 'We'll get you at dinner time,' it said.

The girl knew that it came from skinny Nigel Bennett.

Sharon shivered at the threat then turned her attention to what Miss Dennison was saying. 'Now, Sharon, I was talking about riddles... you know what a riddle is?'

'Yes Miss,' Sharon muttered.

'Let's see if you can guess this one,' the teacher said, turning to an old green book.

She began reading the riddle:

'Riddle me, riddle me, what is that
Over your head and under your hat?'

There was silence in the class for a few moments then Mark Jones stuck his hand in the air.

'Yes, Mark?' Miss Dennison asked.

'Please, Miss, I don't wear a hat,' he said. The boys giggled while Miss Dennison glared, her lips pinched tight.

'Don't be stupid, Mark Jones,' she snapped.

'But I *don't* wear a hat!' the boy tried to argue.

'Mark Jones, you are being deliberately cheeky! You will stay behind for an extra five minutes at lunch time.'

Sharon saw the back of Mark's neck turn red with anger. Suddenly she understood; the boy *wasn't* being cheeky or silly. He really *didn't* understand the question. Sharon thought she would help.

'Please, Miss Dennison, the answer is *hair*.'

Miss Dennison beamed at her, showing her small, sharp teeth. 'Excellent, Sharon, as usual!'

Mark Jones turned and his eyes were narrow with hate. 'Miss Know-it-all,' he whispered. 'Just you *wait*!'

Sharon sighed. She never seemed to say the right thing.

Miss Dennison was going on about riddles. 'Of course some of these riddles are hundreds of years old and they were closely linked with magic spells.'

Sharon jumped. The word 'magic' reminded her of Ellie in the church. 'Miss Dennison... is it true they used to burn witches in olden days?' she asked suddenly.

'Why, yes,' the teacher replied. 'And there are records to show that many were ducked in Inkling pond out there.'

'That's daft... it would put the fire out,' Mark Jones muttered.

'You will now stay behind for *ten* minutes at lunch time, Mark Jones,' Miss Dennison said tartly. The boy gave a low moan. 'As I was saying,' the teacher went on, 'the ducking was a form of witch trial. The witch was tied to a ducking stool – rather like a see-saw with one end over the pond. It was then lowered into the pond. If the witch sank then he or she was innocent.'

'*He* or she,' Nigel Bennett put in. He was a tall, thin boy with a mass of freckles that spread over his button nose. 'You mean the witch could be a man?'

'Oh, yes,' Miss Dennison went on. 'Several men have been burned as witches in Inkling village – or Little Inkling as it used to be known in the Middle Ages.' The teacher placed the green book on her desk and peered over the top of her reading glasses. 'Now, before you begin today's written work, are there any more questions?'

'Nigel,' hissed Mark Jones. 'Ask her where she parks her broomstick when she comes to school!'

Nigel tried to smother his giggle but only made a sound like a sneezing sparrow.

'And you, Nigel Bennett, you will keep your friend Mark company for ten minutes during the lunch break.'

Sharon felt sorry for the boys... but at least she would now have ten minutes start in the race to get back to the church and Ellie.

Sharon ran from the bright September noon into the cool dimness of the church. The clock was striking the last stroke of twelve. 'Ellie!' she called softly. The bramble-bush hair and dusty face appeared from behind the organ stool. 'Come on, let's go!'

'Where to, Miss Sharon?' the six-hundred year old girl asked.

'We want to get you back to your own time,' Sharon explained as she led the way to the door of the church. 'But if you re-appear in the church you might walk straight into Harry Henson's hands. Let's go somewhere near your home and then wish us back there.'

Ellie nodded. 'I see...'

Ellie stopped at the church door. Her eyebrows vanished into the dark mop of hair and her mouth fell open. 'This isn't Little Inkling!' she gasped as she gazed out.

'It's Inkling Village, 2003,' Sharon said, tugging the girl's arm. Ellie followed her down the church path stiffly.

'The houses are so... grand!' she murmured, 'but the air chokes me!'

She stumbled forward till she reached the gate of the churchyard then her muscles finally gave up. 'I must be dead,' she said flatly. 'This is Hell... and that monster is the devil come to devour me!' she said with a small scream.

'Don't be silly – it's only the Hoxley bus,'

Sharon said as the red and cream coach rumbled by. 'Now, Ellie, which direction would your home farm be?' she asked.

Ellie shook her head woodenly.

Sharon sighed and started to coax the girl across the road. She was so busy dragging Ellie over the weird black ribbon of tar that she didn't see the two boys. The first she knew of her danger was when she felt each arm roughly grabbed.

'What shall we do with the little witch, Mark?' the tall thin boy called.

'Duck her in the pond, Nigel,' the tubby one cried.

Ellie watched, open mouthed and terrified as her friend was dragged to the edge of the pond. 'But Sharon,' she whispered. 'You said that they don't punish witches in 2003!'

5

Farmer Nash

Sharon kicked and struggled and made the boys slip at the muddy pond edge. Still, they held her tight.

'Bring that plank!' Barry cried. Nigel dragged an old plank to the water's edge. 'Put it over that rock – like a see-saw,' Barry ordered while Nigel hurried to obey. When the slimy see-saw was complete Barry Potter pushed Sharon onto it. He prodded her with a muddy reed.

'You'll dirty my clothes!' she cried.

'Then walk the plank,' he sneered and prodded some more. Barry Potter stood on the dry end of the plank and slowly forced Sharon out to the end that hovered over the muddy water.

'Jump!' he ordered. 'let's see if you float or sink!'

'Don't be stupid, Barry . . . I'll get wet!' Sharon snapped, trying to sound less frightened than she really was.

Barry's round face split with a cruel grin. 'All I have to do is step off the end of this plank and you'll tip in anyway,' he pointed out.

'Then why don't you?' Sharon asked.

'Yes, Barry, why don't you?' skinny Nigel urged his friend.

'Because then I'll be in trouble for ducking her – but if she steps off the end of her own free will, then there's no one to blame but herself!' Barry explained. 'So . . . jump!'

'No!'

Barry grinned slyly and took a step towards Sharon. With the shift of weight the girl's end of the see-saw bobbed down towards the water. Barry's eyes narrowed to glittering slits. 'Go on . . . jump!' he breathed.

Sharon's mouth was too dry to answer. She just shook her head. Barry took a half step towards her and Sharon's end of the plank dipped till it touched the dark water.

Suddenly a ragged brown bundle rushed down the bank of the pond. Ellie hurtled into the back of Barry Potter and bundled him into the oozing muddy reeds. The girl took Barry's place on the end of the plank. She was much lighter than Sharon, but the weight of the black book kept her end of the plank down – and Sharon's feet out of the water.

As Barry wriggled, face down in the slime and sobbed for Nigel to pull him out, Ellie cried gently, 'Walk back along the plank to me, Miss Sharon!'

Sharon's legs felt weak as she shuffled back to safety. As she reached the dry end of the plank Ellie grabbed her hand and yelled, '1402!'

As suddenly as blinking everything went black.

When Sharon's eyes became used to the darkness she could make out that she was standing by the edge of the old pond. The dead light of a sickle moon showed the church in front of her. But where were the street lights and the colourful windows of the new estate? Had there been a power cut? And where was the noise of the traffic . . . in fact, where was the road? Just a dusty path leading to the church-yard gate and, in the other direction, away into the silent purple hills.

'It's all right, Miss Sharon,' Ellie whispered, squeezing her hand. 'I've saved you from the witchfinders. I've taken you back to my village... to 1402.'

Sharon gave a nervous laugh. 'And I thought I was supposed to be saving *you*!'

'Don't worry, Miss Sharon. We can go back to your time whenever we like – so long as we have this book,' Ellie reminded her.

The thought made Sharon feel better. 'I think *your* danger's greater than mine, Ellie. Those boys wouldn't dare to hurt me really – but from what I've heard of your century I'm afraid Harry Henson *could* have you burned. So, I'll stay in 1402 until I'm sure you're safe.'

'But how will you be able to make sure I'm safe?' Ellie asked.

'By showing the villagers who the *real* witch is,'

Sharon explained. 'First we have to find somewhere safe to make our plans.'

'We could go to our farm,' Ellie offered. She pointed towards the grinning moon which was climbing in the eastern sky.

Sharon nodded then stumbled after her friend along the rough path out of the village.

After half a mile they reached the farm. It was no more than a jumble of wooden sheds giving off the strong smell of animals. A dog started barking and a moment later the door of the farmhouse crashed open. 'Is that you, Ellie?' came a man's voice.

'Yes . . . it's me, Dad,' Ellie called back quickly.

A small man with thin, faded hair stepped into the farmyard. He held an oil lamp above his head and peered at Sharon.

'This is Miss Sharon – from Inkling Hall,' Ellie said.

Farmer Nash grunted. 'Where have you been lass?'

'Harry Henson and some of the men chased me after the storm started,' she explained. 'They said the rain was my fault ... they're saying that I'm a witch!'

'Aye,' Farmer Nash said in a gently whining voice. 'Harry was up here looking for you this evening ...'

Ellie seemed to shrink as her father wrapped an arm around her thin shoulders.

'Where is he now?' she asked trembling softly.

'Come into the kitchen, lass, you're cold,' her father said as he pulled her towards the house.

'Where's Henson?' Ellie repeated, and her voice was shrill now.

'If you're not a witch then you have nothing to be afraid of,' the farmer murmured softly and he tightened his grip on her shoulder.

Suddenly Ellie struggled free. She backed away from her father. 'Henson's in the house ... isn't he?' she cried.

Farmer Nash held out a hand to her. He murmured like a mother to a child frightened by a nightmare. 'Nothing to be afraid of.'

Ellie ran to Sharon and pulled her sleeve. 'Into the barn, Miss Sharon. We'll be safe in there,' she cried.

Farmer Nash turned furiously and called towards the lamplit door of the farmhouse. 'She's here, Harry! The little witch is here!'

Sharon and Ellie slithered and whirled over a farmyard still damp from the evening's storm. They raced through the barn doors and swung them shut. Ellie tugged a heavy bar across and sank down with her back to the door.

The barn was dark and silent apart from the squeaks and scutters of the rats in the hay. The girls waited in the damp dark until they heard the sounds that they had been waiting for. The heavy squelching steps of the men.

The door rattled.

'Ellie!' It was her father's voice.

'Let *me* try the door!' That was Henson's voice. A moment later there was a crash. The door cracked and splintered. The barn shuddered.

'You'll wreck my barn!' Farmer Nash whined.

'Better a wrecked barn than a witch-child roaming through it!' came a third voice. Sharon felt truly afraid for the first time. She knew without Ellie telling her that the voice was Father Seyton's.

A second thundering blow shook Sharon.

'No, no, Harry!' Ellie's father pleaded. 'Give her time! She'll come out when she's hungry . . . give her till morning before you break down the barn door.'

'We don't want to give her the chance to do one of her devilish disappearing tricks again,' Father Seyton said. 'We'll give her just one hour to come out . . . then we'll save the trouble of a witch trial.' The priest's voice was as cold and sharp as broken glass when he called through the barn door, 'Hear this, Eleanor Nash . . . if you do not step out to face a fair trial before your hour is up then we'll judge you guilty. We'll burn the barn and you in it!'

'All my hay . . .' Farmer Nash began to object.

'Silence! Or you'll burn with your witch-child,' the priest roared. 'One hour, Eleanor Nash. One hour!'

'Go away!' the frail girl tried to shout, but her voice was as weak as the rustling of reeds.

And the angry footsteps faded into the night.

6

The Black Book

Ellie fumbled in the dark until she found a lantern. She sparked it into life with a small flint she carried in the pocket of her rough brown dress.

The smoky yellow light didn't make the barn any warmer but it made Sharon feel a little happier. The light even seemed to keep the rats away.

'What do we do now?' Ellie asked, her eyes shining with fear.

'We could use the book to escape,' Sharon suggested.

'But where would I go?' Ellie said sadly. 'How would I live in another age? Where would I find food or shelter or work?'

'You could live in 2003 with me – my mum and dad would look after you,' Sharon offered.

Ellie seemed to shrink at the thought. She shook her head. 'Too many monsters,' she said quietly.

'That was a *bus*!' Sharon sighed.

'And all those gallows in the streets – you must hang a lot of people in your age,' Ellie said with a shiver.

'Gallows?' Sharon said.

'Yes,' Ellie replied. She quickly sketched in the dust of the barn floor what she had seen in 2003.

'Oh! Street lamps!' Sharon cried. 'They're nothing to be afraid of!'

But Ellie just shook her head silently.

'Well, we'll have to make sure we don't go to 1603 or 1943 – they were really awful!' Sharon said.

'I want to stay here,' Ellie said.

'Even though they might try to burn you as a witch?' Sharon asked.

'I'm not a witch,' Ellie said in a low but firm voice.

Sharon shrugged. 'Then we'll just have to prove it, I suppose.'

Ellie nodded. 'You said you knew who the witch was – if you *could* prove it . . .'

'Yes, I do know, if what you told me was right . . . and I *can* prove it . . . but I'm not sure that the villagers will really believe it,' Sharon said with a frown. Ellie looked at her with her trusting blue eyes. Sharon knew she couldn't let her down. She forced a smile and said, 'We'll just have to *make* them believe it, won't we?'

Ellie's small mouth turned up at the corners. It was the first time that Sharon had seen her smile. 'How do you know who the witch is, Miss Sharon?' she asked.

Sharon took the black book from the straw and tried to explain slowly. 'Witches used to think that if you take something holy and turn it backwards or upside down . . . I mean, if you want to call the devil

you must say the Lord's Prayer backwards – or you
take the sign of the cross and you turn it the wrong
way round.' Sharon pointed to the gold cross on the
front of the black book. It was upside down. 'See?
That's how I knew it wasn't a bible.'

'But it must be! I took it from the lectern in the
church!' Ellie cried. Sharon just nodded. 'But if it
isn't a bible, then what is it?' Ellie asked.

'Probably a spell book. Let's look,' Sharon said.

'I can't read,' Ellie said.

'Don't worry... I'm the best reader in my class,'
Sharon boasted... then she bit her lip. That was the
sort of silly thing she was always saying. No wonder
Mark Jones hated her, she thought. Then, when she
had opened the crackling yellow pages, she felt still
more foolish.

'What does the writing say, Miss Sharon?' she asked eagerly.

Sharon blushed crimson red in the smoky light. 'I don't know,' she said slowly.

'I thought you could read,' Ellie said.

'Ah ... yes ... but ...' Sharon stammered. 'This is written in Latin.'

'Of course,' Ellie said. 'All the church services are in Latin.'

'You understand them?' Sharon asked.

'Oh, no ... Father Seyton reads them in Latin then tells us what they mean. Can't you do that?' Ellie asked.

'No,' Sharon muttered, half ashamed. She turned the brittle pages miserably.

The ink was faded to brown, but the pictures, painted in brilliant colours, shone. Magic signs and symbols ... drawings of dragons, with scales greener than grass, breathing red-gold flames that seemed to burn the page. There were unicorns with silvered horns and bronzed eagles – Sharon knew them. But most of the creatures were straight out of Sharon's worst nightmares – ugly and gruesome, evil and threatening.

She turned quickly past these and came to the last part of the frightening book. The ink here was blacker, newer – and the writing was in English ... strange and old, with odd spellings, but still English. Sharon wanted to prove she could read.

'Here's a spell,' she said quickly. 'It is to protect you from the anger of your enemies!'

'That's what I need,' Ellie said hopefully. 'What do I have to do?'

'It's a poem,' Sharon said and began to read.

'*I am not a shield – but I turn away spite;*
I have many fine teeth – yet I never bite;
I'm as red as the sky when dawn's nearly come;
I'm the shape of the moon – but I'm warm as
the sun.'

Sharon put the book down and chewed at a ragged fingernail. Ellie waited quietly for a while then said, 'That's very clever, Miss Sharon, thank you – I wish I could read.'

'It's a riddle,' Sharon said.

'I know,' Ellie replied.

'I'm usually very good at riddles,' Sharon told her.

'Good?'

'Yes. I can usually work out what they mean,' Sharon said. 'But this one's ... er ...'

'Easy,' Ellie said.

Sharon was astonished. 'Is it?'

'Oh, yes,' Ellie said. 'We tell each other riddles all the time – it's a good game to play by the fireside on long winter nights.'

'Then what does it mean?' Sharon asked. A spell to protect her from the anger of Mark Jones was just what she needed.

'Don't you know?' Ellie asked.

'No,' Sharon snapped. She was just a little cross that someone who couldn't even read could be cleverer than she was. But perhaps that's *exactly* how Mark Jones felt about her, she realised. It *is* annoying to have someone make you look silly by showing their own cleverness – and Sharon did it all the time in class. Now it was happening to her and she musn't let it spoil her friendship with Ellie. She sighed a little and took a deep, calming breath. 'Sorry, Ellie – I'm not as good at riddles as I thought I was. What is the answer?'

'Oh, the answer is . . . what's that?' Ellie swung round sharply and scrambled to her feet.

'What's what?'

'I can smell smoke!' Ellie breathed.

And in the quietness Sharon could hear the soft crackle of burning. 'They've set fire to the barn!' she cried. 'They're going to burn us alive!'

Sharon rushed to the door and slid back the bar. Together the girls pushed at the door.

Someone had jammed it shut.

7

The Witch

Smoke curled through cracks in the planks of the barn. It stung Sharon's eyes to tears. A spark floated through the sooty air and settled on the dry straw. Sharon gave a gasp and stamped quickly on the flicker of fire before it grew and swallowed them.

'The book,' Ellie cried. 'We have to use the book to escape!'

As Sharon stretched a hand out to touch the book she heard a shout from outside the barn.

'Water! Fetch water!' It was Ellie's father. 'Father Seyton,' he went on, 'we agreed to give the child an hour to come out and stand trial!'

'We'll smoke the witch-child out,' Father Seyton roared.

'Then you can pay for a new barn and a hundred bales of hay,' Farmer Nash argued.

Before the priest could answer Sharon heard the sound of running feet and the spitting of water on the flames.

Soon the thick grey smoke turned to white steam and faded into the rafters of the barn. The heavy barn doors swung slowly open and a dozen crackling torches lit the angry faces of the villagers of Little Inkling.

Father Seyton's blood-shot eyes bulged when he saw the book in Ellie's clutches. 'Burn the witches!' he roared and the line of smoking torches moved closer.

'Wait!' Sharon said, stepping boldly forward to meet the crowd. The line of torches stopped. 'Eleanor Nash is not a witch . . . and I can prove it!'

'Ellie Nash *is* a witch – and we don't need any more proof!' a fat man snarled. His face and bare arms were the colour of raw beef.

'That's Blacksmith Henson,' Ellie whispered at Sharon's shoulder.

'We were in the church – we saw her disappear,' Harry Henson was saying. 'If that's not witchcraft then tell me what is!'

'That wasn't Ellie's witchcraft – it was the power of this book!' Sharon cried. She tugged the black book from Ellie's grasp and held it in the air.

'That's the Bible,' Henson growled. 'The Bible the little witch took from the church when she vanished.'

'No,' Sharon said holding the book open. 'Look! It's a book of witchcraft.'

Henson backed away from the book – afraid yet angry. 'That's the word of God there! Give it back to the priest you devil-child!'

'Just *read* it!' Sharon urged.

Henson turned an even deeper shade of brick red. 'I can't read,' he muttered. 'What would a blacksmith want with reading?'

Sharon thrust the book at some of the other villagers. The reply was always the same. 'Can't read.'

'Give it to Father Seyton,' Farmer Nash said.

'That's right. The priest can read,' Harry Henson agreed.

Sharon held the book towards Father Seyton and torch light flickered on his grey teeth as he reached forward greedily to take it from her. 'No! Don't touch it!' Sharon said quickly. 'Just *read* it.'

The priest shrugged. He leaned forward, his mouth spreading in a cunning smile. He peered at the book. He turned to the crowd and in a clear voice said simply, 'It's the Bible.'

The villagers muttered threats against the girls and the circle of lights began to close around them.

'He's lying!' Sharon cried.

'Priests don't lie,' Henson said.

'Why should he want to lie?' Farmer Nash put in.

'He's lying to save himself!' Sharon shouted.

Some of the villagers chuckled uneasily.

'Save himself from what?' an old woman in a red shawl asked.

'Save himself from being burned as a witch!' Sharon replied.

'Eeeh!' the little woman gasped. Her mouth hung open in shock showing the black stumps that were once teeth.

'That's Granny Rickles,' Ellie muttered in Sharon's ear.

'You're not trying to tell us that the good Father Seyton's a witch, are you?' the old woman asked.

'If you are lying then you'll burn with Ellie Nash,' Harry Henson threatened, 'even if you are a guest at his lordship's manor.'

'You can look in the church,' Sharon said. 'Witches take holy things and turn them upside down or back to front . . .'

'We know that, lass,' Granny Rickles put in.

'Then look at the altar cross – it's loose – Ellie saw Father Seyton moving it when she ran into the church this evening,' Sharon told the villagers.

'The cross is loose,' Father Seyton said quickly. 'I was trying to mend it.' His voice was soft and easy but his eyes were bulging.

'What about this book?' the girl said.

'A Bible!' the priest argued.

'Then why is the cross upside down?'

'The monks made a mistake!'

'And how do you explain black candles in the church?' Sharon asked.

'Black candles?' Father Seyton said with a choking laugh.

'Black candles!' Harry Henson said in his deeply rumbling voice. 'That's a sure sign of witchcraft.'

'There are no black candles in my church!' Father Seyton cried. He ran a frightened tongue over his red, wet lips.

Ellie stepped forward. 'I remember! He pushed them behind the choir seats!' she said excitedly. 'I wondered why he was trying to hide them.'

'The priest hasn't been out of our sight since then,' Henson said, turning to the villagers. 'If the girl is right then they'll still be there.'

'I'll go and look!' Farmer Nash offered.

'We'll all go!' someone in the crowd shouted. 'If the girl's right then we'll come back and deal with Seyton later.'

'And we'd better take that devil's book with us,' Henson said. 'Leave it in the church where it can't do any harm.' Before Sharon knew what was happening the big man had snatched the black book from her hands and was leading the line of torches back to the village.

Soon the only light was the orange pool round Ellie's lamp; the only sound the gentle hissing of charred timber; the only people at Nash farm, Ellie, Sharon and Father Seyton.

The priest pulled nervously at his greasy beard. 'They'll burn me,' he muttered.

'Yes,' Ellie said quietly. 'That's what you told them should happen to a witch.'

'But I wasn't a very good witch ... have a little pity on a poor old man,' he whined.

'You ought to burn,' Ellie said simply. 'That is the law.'

Sharon rested a hand on Ellie's arm. 'But it's a very hard law, Ellie. He's not a really bad man ... just a stupid one.'

Seyton nodded weakly. 'It was only the book that had power ... I found it hidden beneath the church floor ... it could have been there hundreds of years.'

'Some of the writing was quite new,' Sharon pointed out.

Father Seyton shrugged. 'A few simple charms I added myself – riddles, not magic spells. Not enough to deserve to burn.'

Sharon sighed. 'I suppose if you ran away from us now we couldn't really stop you.'

Seyton's eyes shone craftily. He began to back away into the darkness. Sharon and Ellie said nothing. The faded black of his gown was lost in the misty air. Red eyes and red lips glowed in the sickly white face for a few moments longer, then they too were gone.

Ellie sighed. 'I hope he escapes. No matter how cruel he was to me, I couldn't bear to see him suffer. Poor Father Seyton.'

'Not Seyton,' Sharon said softly, 'but Satan.'

Ellie was quiet for a long time then she turned to Sharon with a shy smile. 'You did what you promised,' she said. 'You saved me from burning.'

But Sharon wasn't smiling. In a dead voice she said, 'And without the book I'm trapped six hundred years in my own past.'

8

Inkling Church

Sharon and Ellie hurried down the muddy path towards the church. 'Henson said he'd put the book in the church,' Ellie panted.

They reached the edge of the village. It was an hour since the villagers had returned to the Nash farm howling for Father Seyton's blood. They had found the black candles and much, much more in the church. They were sure that the priest had studied witchcraft.

When Ellie told them that he had escaped they set off on a wild search of the hills. The circle of torches around Little Inkling spread out like ripples on a pond. But the heart of the village was dark apart from a single candle-lit window.

'That's Joseph the Reeve's house,' Ellie explained as they hurried past. 'He works for Lord Inkling. A very clever man. He can even read.'

Sharon just nodded. She was too worried to chatter with her friend. Ellie, on the other hand, was as happy as a rabbit in a carrot field. She was at home in her own time and free, at last, from the threat of burning.

The girls turned in at the church gate. They tried to shut their ears to the ghostly sighing of the wind in the yew trees. They turned their eyes from the gravestones glimmering in the weak moonlight.

Ellie lit the two lamps she had brought from the farm. They cast huge swirling shadows around the church walls as the girls moved down the aisle. The straw on the floor rustled under their feet. Sharon went straight to the lectern and pulled the large black book towards her. 'Do you think it will work for me?' she asked.

Ellie shrugged. 'It doesn't matter. I'll go with you. I can bring the book back and we'll both be in our own times again,' she said.

Ellie grasped the book. Sharon held Ellie's hand and closed her eyes.

'Two thousand and three!' Ellie breathed.

Sharon opened her eyes. She was still in the church – and it was night here too. She stepped forward and her heart seemed to jump into her throat.

For under her feet she felt the soft crackle of straw.

Inkling Village church of 2003 didn't have straw on the floor.

'It didn't work!' she said flatly and she felt faint. If she had opened her eyes and seen Mark Jones waiting to duck her then she would have run up to him and cuddled him. Anything, even Mark Jones, would be better than being trapped in the cruel world of 1402.

'I'll try again,' Ellie said. This time she cried in a loud voice that echoed round the empty stone walls. 'Two thousand and three!'

Nothing.

And still the straw on the floor.

Sharon flung the book open and looked at the first page. It was in Latin... but she understood the title at the top. 'Genesis,' she muttered. 'Genesis!' She turned back to the cross on the cover. It was the right way up. 'A Bible!' she cried. 'This is a real Bible!' Sharon didn't know whether to laugh at the silliness of her mistake or panic at the loss of the witchcraft book.

'This isn't Father Seyton's black book then?' Ellie asked.

'No. We'll have to search the church.' Sharon said.

But thirty minutes later, with every corner explored the girls had found eighty-eight knee cushions, twenty-seven bottles of wine and thirteen mouse-holes – but no book of spells.

'But Harry Henson said he was putting the book in the church,' Ellie said.

'Then Harry Henson lied,' Sharon said bitterly.

'But what use is it to him? He can't even read it,' Ellie argued.

Sharon chewed her lip, thinking hard. 'The candle in the window,' she said, half to herself.

But Ellie understood. 'Of course! Joseph the Reeve can read! Henson could have gone to him!'

'Then we'll have to go there too, if we want the book,' Sharon said grimly.

The girls tiptoed to the window and slowly raised their noses above the windowsill. They saw two men sitting at a table. The broad bull back of Henson was turned to them while a thin grey man faced them.

'The Reeve and Henson,' Ellie breathed. Sharon nodded silently. The voices of the two men drifted carelessly through the open window.

'So, it's not a book of spells?' Henson was saying.

'Not exactly. There are a few simple charms at the back of the book. They must have been stuck in by that fool Seyton. Clearly he didn't understand the real power of this book,' the Reeve answered in a sour voice. 'These front pages seem to be a thousand years old or more!'

'Then tell me ... what *is* the real power of the book?' Henson said, excited.

'It appears to give the owner the power to travel through time.' the Reeve answered.

'Pfah! Is that all?' Henson sneered. 'What good is that? How can we become rich with that?'

The Reeve looked down his long thin nose at the blacksmith and said in a sharp voice, 'You are clearly an even bigger fool than Seyton.'

Henson rose to his feet and leaned forward angrily. 'Then *you* tell me, Mister Clever Reeve, what profit there is in being able to travel through time!'

'I have not had time to think about it, but some simple ideas do occur to me . . .' the Reeve said in his slow, sneering voice.

'Such as?'

'Such as . . . we could go into the future, see what will happen there, and come back to tell the people.

We would be hailed as the world's greatest and truest prophets!'

Henson sank slowly into his seat. The Reeve went on, 'We could tell the farmers what the weather will be like next week . . . or next year . . . or for the next hundred years. They could store food for the bad years and sell it for a lot of money. They would become rich that way . . . and so would we because we would sell them this knowledge.'

Henson grunted. 'Farmers are careful folk. It would take them years to see our prophecies come true. Isn't there a quicker way to get rich?'

The Reeve shrugged. 'Of course we could always go forwards or backwards in time and steal something from another age. Then we can vanish into the safety of our own age where the law could never find us!'

Henson jumped to his feet again. This time he seemed excited. 'Yes' he hissed. 'That's more like it!' He snatched the book from the table.

'Where are you going with that?' the Reeve asked sharply.

'I'm going to look after it at my cottage,' Henson said.

'I need to study it!' the Reeve said.

'You can study it when I'm with you,' Henson said.

'Don't you trust me?' the Reeve snapped.

Henson gave a low, nasty chuckle. 'No.' He tucked the book under his arm and turned to go. 'I'll see you tomorrow at cock-crow – and then we'll start to steal the world!'

Henson strode into the night with the book held tightly under his fat arm. The girls slid into the safe shadow of a bush while he passed. Without needing to say a word they stood up and followed him.

Henson's cottage was as dirty and tattered as Granny Rickles' poor home. The girls peered through a rip in the moth-eaten curtain; they watched as Henson put the black book under his pillow, threw himself onto the bed and blew out his candle.

'Now what can I do?' Sharon moaned.

'We'll just go in and take the book,' Ellie said simply.

9

The Riddle

'Just like that?' Sharon said. She felt bitter and helpless. The words came out with a sneer, but Ellie didn't seem to notice.

'Just like that,' Ellie replied. 'Wait here.'

She slipped away silently and Sharon shivered alone. The only sound was the grating snore of Henson inside the cottage.

When Ellie returned five minutes later she was clutching something dark, wriggling and squeaking in each hand. 'Bats,' she said. 'They live in Henson's barn.'

'But why do we want bats?' Sharon asked.

And Ellie whispered her plan into Sharon's ear.

Two minutes later Ellie lifted the wooden latch and the girls slipped into the room. When Sharon had taken her place at the foot of Henson's bed Ellie set the bats free.

As the bats squeaked and clattered around the dark room Henson stirred. 'What's that?' he mumbled in a slurred and sleepy tone.

Ellie put on a high, creaking voice. 'Harry Henson!' she cried. 'Harry Henson!'

'Who's that?' Henson croaked, and he sounded very frightened.

Sharon used the voice she had used as the witch in the school play. 'Harry Henson! Harry Henson!'

To the half-awake Henson the voices seemed to be coming from all corners of the room. The scratching of bat claws on his face made him gasp.

'What do you want?' he cried.

'Where's my book?' Ellie cackled.

'Where's my book?' Sharon echoed.

'Who are you?' the blacksmith asked and his voice was shaking.

'Guess,' Ellie hissed.

'Guess.'

'Did the devil send you for his book?' Henson whined.

Ellie gave such a blood-curdling laugh that even Sharon shivered in the dark.

Henson fumbled under the pillow and flung the book onto the floor with a heavy thud. The noise and the cloud of dust sent the bats into a new frenzy of screeching.

Ellie scrambled for the book and wrapped her hands around it.

'Never meddle with magic, Henson,' she warned.

'No, no! ... I won't!' Henson gabbled. 'Never again, I promise! Never-never-never!' He pulled the bedclothes over his head and sobbed. And the blacksmith didn't come out from under them until the sun was high in the autumn sky the next day.

Sharon saw a square of starlight when Ellie opened the door. She hurried towards the fresh air, away from the choking smell of dust and stale food.

The bats just beat her to it.

The girls ran past the dark pond towards the church. They were gasping and laughing in the same breath. When they had recovered they planned their next step through time. 'If we're in the church when we leave 1402 then we should arrive in the church in 2003,' Sharon said as they stood at the door.

'That seems to be the way it works,' Ellie agreed.

'What day, though? And what time will we arrive?' Sharon wondered. It wouldn't do to arrive in Inkling Village a week before she left it – there would be two Sharon Neales wandering around in 2003! Or what if she didn't arrive back till a month *after* she left? Her parents would be worried witless for that month.

'Maybe we can control the book,' Ellie said.

Sharon shrugged. 'We've got nothing to lose,' she said. 'Tell the book to take us to Wednesday the ninth of September, at four o'clock.'

Sharon and Ellie joined hands in the dark of Little Inkling Church. Ellie said in a clear voice, 'Four o'clock on Wednesday, September the ninth, two thousand and three.'

Sharon blinked as the strong afternoon sunlight flooded into Inkling Village church. Above her head the clock in the tower began to chime four. She sighed and turned to Ellie. 'Oh, thank you, Ellie. Thank you!'

'No, Miss Sharon. It's I who should be thanking you ... you saved me from Henson. I don't think he'll be bothering me again,' Ellie said. 'I only wish I could repay you in some way.'

As the last chime of the clock struck, Sharon lowered her head and looked up shyly at Ellie. 'There's one thing ...'

'Anything!' Ellie urged.

'It's silly ... you'll laugh ...' Sharon said, stumbling to find the right words.

'Promise I won't,' Ellie said.

'Well ... There are two boys who ... who *hate* me ... and that black book has a riddle to protect people from the anger of their enemies. Could you tell me what it means ... please?'

Slowly Ellie's face broke into a broad grin – the ivory white of her teeth glowed brightly in the oak brown of her face.

Sharon turned red. 'You promised not to laugh,' she snapped.

'Oh, but I'm not,' Ellie cried. 'You don't understand. Read the riddle again.'

Sharon took the book and turned to the back.

'*I am not a shield, but I turn away spite,*' she read. 'That's what I need,' she murmured. '*I have many fine teeth – yet I never bite,*' she went on. 'How can it protect me from Mark Jones if it can't use its teeth to bite him?' Sharon wondered. '*I'm as red as the sun when dawn's nearly come...* well that could be almost anything! It could be a beetroot or a rose or a

61

dragon!' she sighed. 'I'm the shape of the moon but as warm as the sun,' she finished and shook her head sadly.

Ellie's mouth opened into a warm, crescent-moon smile.

'You're smiling again,' Sharon said.

'Because that is the answer to the riddle,' Ellie said.

'A smile!' Sharon gasped. 'Well... yes it does have teeth but it doesn't bite; and I suppose it is moon-shaped and lips *are* red... but if Mark Jones is being spiteful I can't turn around and... and *smile* at him! Can I?'

Ellie didn't answer the question. She simply said, 'Goodbye, Miss Sharon – and good luck!' Then she stretched out her hands and took back the book. '1402!' she said.

Ellie flickered into nothingness. Sharon was left with only the memory of her warm smile.

'Goodbye, Ellie,' she whispered.

10

Inkling Pond

Eleanor Nash stepped wearily from the church of Little Inkling into the grey-blue early light of the 1402 morning. She wandered down to the edge of the smooth, silver pond.

The sun hadn't risen yet but the air was already warm. It was going to be a fine, hot day. Maybe the hay crop could be saved after all. Now that Little Inkling was rid of its witch, perhaps the luck of the villagers would change.

But there was one thing still left to do. Ellie waded out into the cool, shining pool till the water rose above her knees. Gathering all her strength, she flung the book into the middle of the pond.

The ripples soon faded and once again the pool was as smooth as a cloudless sky.

'You can stay there until the end of time,' Ellie murmured. She turned and ran lightly up the path to her home.

And the black book settled into the weeds and silt of Little Inkling pond with only the fish and the frogs to read its evil secrets. And there it stayed for hundreds of years, though *not* till the end of time!

Sharon Neale slipped quietly through the door

of the Inkling Village church into the autumn sun of a 2003 evening.

The village green was filled with flashing lights of amber and blue. Men in navy beetled around the police cars, ambulance and fire engines. Men in black with flippers on their feet paddled and plunged in the weedy water of Inkling Village pond. Men with cameras and notebooks and microphones jostled for the best view of the pond; they trampled the reeds and the late-summer flowers.

It seemed that everyone in Inkling and people from miles around had come to watch the excitement. Sharon stood on tiptoe to peer over the shoulders of the crowd. 'What are they doing?' she asked an old lady at the edge.

'Looking for a young girl – disappeared about dinner time – they're dragging the pond for her now!' the old lady gabbled.

Sharon felt a sudden panic. It could be one of her friends down in the depths of that black water! 'What's her name?' she asked.

'Oh ... Sharon ... something,' the old woman muttered, stretching to get a better view. Sharon swallowed hard.

'Not ... not Sharon *Neale*?'

'Aye, that's it. Sharon Neale ... poor lass,' the old woman said. 'I hope they find her before it gets dark. I have to get home to make my Albert's tea ...' she went on.

But Sharon wasn't listening. She felt relieved – and very foolish. How on earth was she going to explain this? For, if she told the truth, who on earth would believe her?

Suddenly there was a shout from the pond side.

'Ah! They've found the body!' the old woman said and her eyes glittered hopefully.

A diver ploughed his way out of the pond with something black and dripping in his arms.

A murmur ran through the crowd. Disappointment. 'Only a book,' someone said. 'Just an old black book!'

The diver showed it to a policeman. They shook their heads for a few moments then threw the book back into the water.

And there it might *really* stay until the end of time.

Then Sharon saw her parents standing by a police caravan. They looked scared and unhappy. She pushed her way through the crowd and ran towards them.

But who was going to believe the truth?

11

Inkling School

Miss Dennison frowned and looked sternly over the top of her glasses at Sharon.

'Well, young lady, you seem to have caused a lot of people a lot of heartache and a lot of trouble.'

Sharon waited for the giggle of glee from Barry Potter. But he sat silent, staring at his desk.

'Well, Sharon? What have you to say for yourself?'

Barry Potter looked up sharply. Sharon glanced over and caught his eye. His fat face was white with panic. Then she understood his misery. Of course! If she told the truth about Barry's attempt to duck her then he would be in terrible trouble.

'I went to the church,' Sharon said slowly and truthfully.

'Why?' Miss Dennison rapped.

'Because I didn't want to come to school,' the girl said choosing her words carefully. She didn't want to lie . . . but she didn't want to put any blame on Barry or Nigel.

'What's wrong with school?' the teacher demanded.

Sharon was silent for a few moments. Then she

added quietly but clearly, 'I just didn't feel like coming.'

There was a gasp of horror and surprise from the class. 'How dare you!' Miss Dennison stormed, launching into a five-minute lecture on how lucky the children were to have a school like Inkling School. 'In olden times children didn't even *have* a school to go to!'

'I know, Miss,' Sharon said with a slight smile.

'And *how* do you know?' Miss Dennison asked. 'Because Inkling School taught you!'

'No, Miss,' Sharon said. She was about to go on, 'Because I've been back in time and seen for myself,' but she stopped herself halfway.

'Don't back-answer,' Miss Dennison rapped. Then she said, 'Nigel Bennett ... you sit in Sharon Neale's seat ... and you, Miss Neale can sit here at the front of the class – next to Barry Potter!' As

Sharon sat next to the pale boy, Miss Dennison turned to the class. 'Now, Class Four, open your books at page 17. Today we are going to look at anagrams.'

While the class rustled on to their work Sharon settled into her new seat. Miss Dennison began to explain the work and Barry Potter leaned carefully towards Sharon. 'Oh, no... here we go!' Sharon thought.

To her surprise he whispered, 'Thanks, mate!'

Sharon turned to him and her smile was the shape of the moon but warm as the sun and red as the dawn. 'Anytime... mate!' she answered.

Barry Potter gave a shy, small grin in return.

'Sharon Neale!' Miss Dennison snapped. 'You are talking! You will stay behind for ten minutes at lunchtime!'

'Yes, Miss,' Sharon said with a shrug.

'Now then, Class Four – who can tell me what an anagram is?' the teacher asked, standing behind her desk.

Sharon was about to shoot up her hand... but stopped so as to give her class-mates a chance to answer first. She knew that part of her wanted to prove she was smarter than her class-mates. And that was cruel.

Jane Argyle raised a timid hand. 'Miss Dennison... I think it's when you take the letters of one word and change them around to make a new word.'

'Very good, Jane!' Miss Dennison beamed. 'I'll give you a simple example – take the letters of the word CAT... C – A – T. Change the letters around and you come up with the word ACT! Now you try. Take the word TEAM – what other word could you make from the letters T – E – A – M?'

Sharon thought quickly. From the corner of her mouth she whispered a word to Barry Potter.

Barry's hand shot up. 'Please, Miss – the word MATE!'

Miss Dennison looked surprised but pleased.

'And MEAT!' Sharon murmured so that only Mark could hear.

'And MEAT!' Barry added.

Miss Dennison blinked.

'And TAME,' Sharon breathed.

'And TAME!' Barry called.

'That really is very good indeed, Barry Potter! There is hope for you yet!'

Barry pulled a face but couldn't hide the fact that he was pleased with the praise.

And Sharon felt as happy as if Miss Dennison had praised *her*. In fact, Sharon realised with a small shock that it felt even better!

Of course Ellie would have known that, she thought. Ellie knew about helping others. After all, Ellie had risked everything to help Sharon steal the black book from Henson's room. Ellie even helped the people who'd been cruel to her – Sharon remembered how she allowed Seyton to escape, then sent the villagers off in the wrong direction.

'That's how I'll have to help Barry Potter,' Sharon decided.

'Yes,' Sharon thought. 'In future I'll try to be more like Ellie is...' Then with a shock she realised she meant, 'More like Ellie *was*... for Ellie's been dead for more than six hundred years!' The thought brought a stinging tear to her eye.

'No! Ellie can't be dead,' she said to herself. 'I was with her yesterday in Inkling Church... that's it! She was alive yesterday and she's *still* alive – she just happens to be alive in some other time!'

The jangling bell brought Sharon's thoughts back into the classroom. Through the clattering of the class leaving the classroom Barry muttered, 'Bad luck, Sharon – Miss Dennison picking on you like that.'

Sharon smiled. 'Never mind – I'll get used to it.'

Still Barry hung back. 'Yesterday... that girl with the wild brown hair...'

'What about her?' Sharon asked. She was hoping that Barry wasn't going to ask who she was.

'Well... she pushed me in the pond... and by the time Nigel had pulled me out of the mud, you'd vanished... I was afraid that I'd drowned you.'

'No,' Sharon said quickly. 'We just ran off very fast.'

Barry's pale face showed spots of red on the cheeks. 'Well... I was glad to see you this morning,' he said blushing even more. 'There was a time when I thought I'd never see you again!'

Sharon gave a thoughtful smile. 'And there were times when I thought I'd never see you again,' she said and she shuddered as she remembered how the real Bible had failed to bring her back to 2003.

'Well... I'm sorry,' Barry muttered before he turned to hurry off.

Miss Dennison loomed over Sharon's desk. 'Now, Miss Neale, as a punishment you can sit there for five minutes and ... and do an anagram for me. An anagram of the name SHARON NEALE!'

Sharon took a piece of paper and jotted down the letters of her name in alphabetical order.

A – A – E – E – H – L – N – N – O – R – S,

She stared at the letters blankly. Sharon could see only simple, short words – son, ran, heel ...

Then she stared so hard and so long that the

letters began to swim in front of her eyes. Perhaps it was the heat of the September sun beating through the window... or perhaps a little six-hundred-year-old magic... but the letters blurred and then two words seemed to stand out clearly.

Sharon blinked. Then she smiled. A smile as warm as the sun and as red as the sky when dawn's nearly come.

It even thawed Miss Dennison's frosty face. 'Well, Sharon... have you made a word from the letters of your name?'

'Yes, Miss Dennison... or should I say I've made *two* words... another name in fact!'

'Really? What name is that?'

'It's a girl's name. It's a girl I knew six hundred years ago – I met her yesterday.' Sharon looked up into the cross and puzzled face of the teacher.

'You see, the letters of SHARON NEALE... spell ELEANOR NASH!'

Sharon laughed softly and looked through the classroom window. She could see the old pond, cool and bright in its dusty hollow.

Slowly the pond sucked the secret book back into its silent water.

Never again would an Inkling witch-child travel through time.

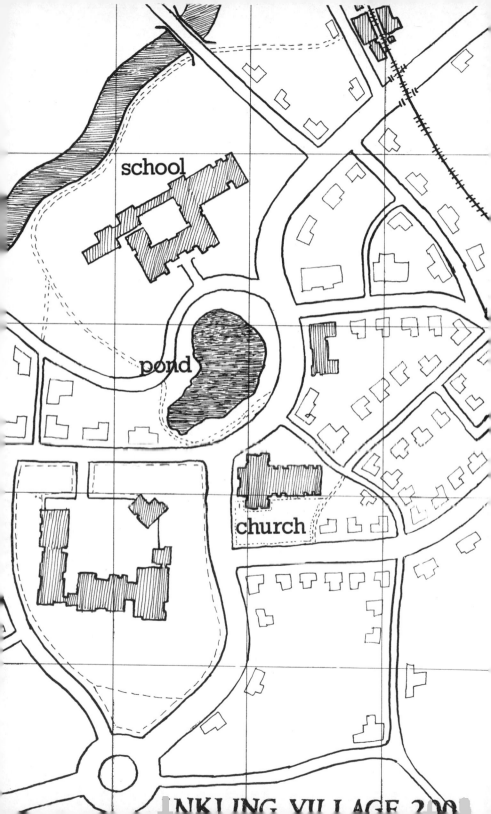

school

pond

church

INKLING VILLAGE 2000